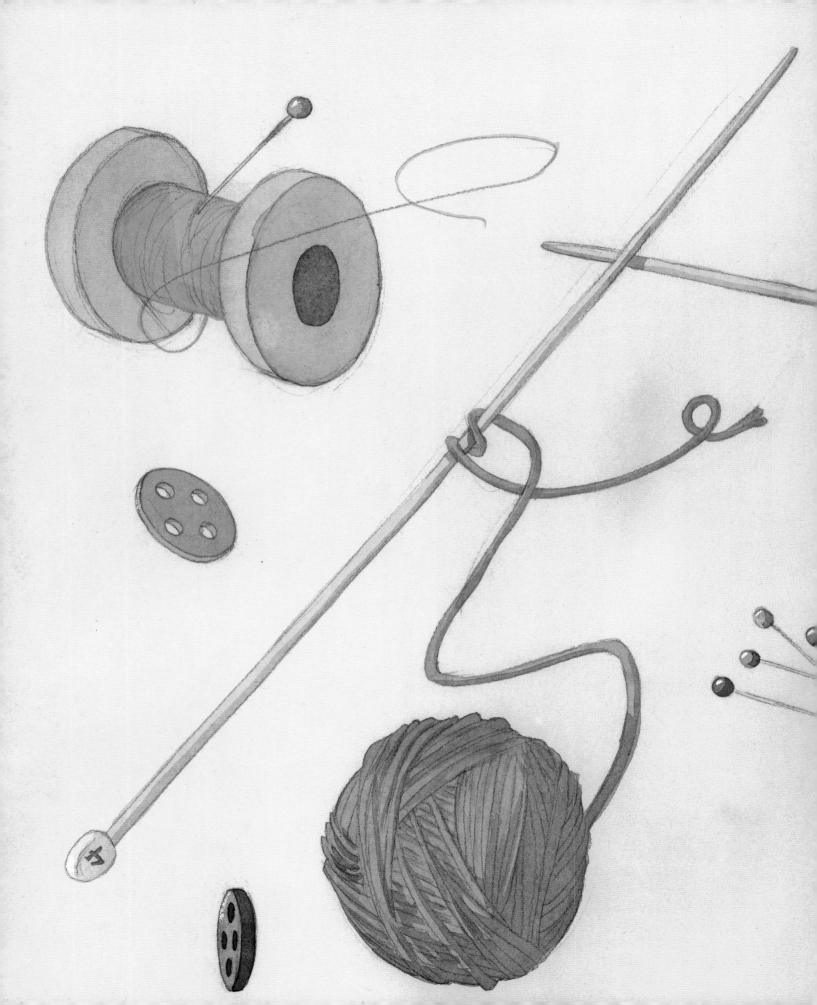

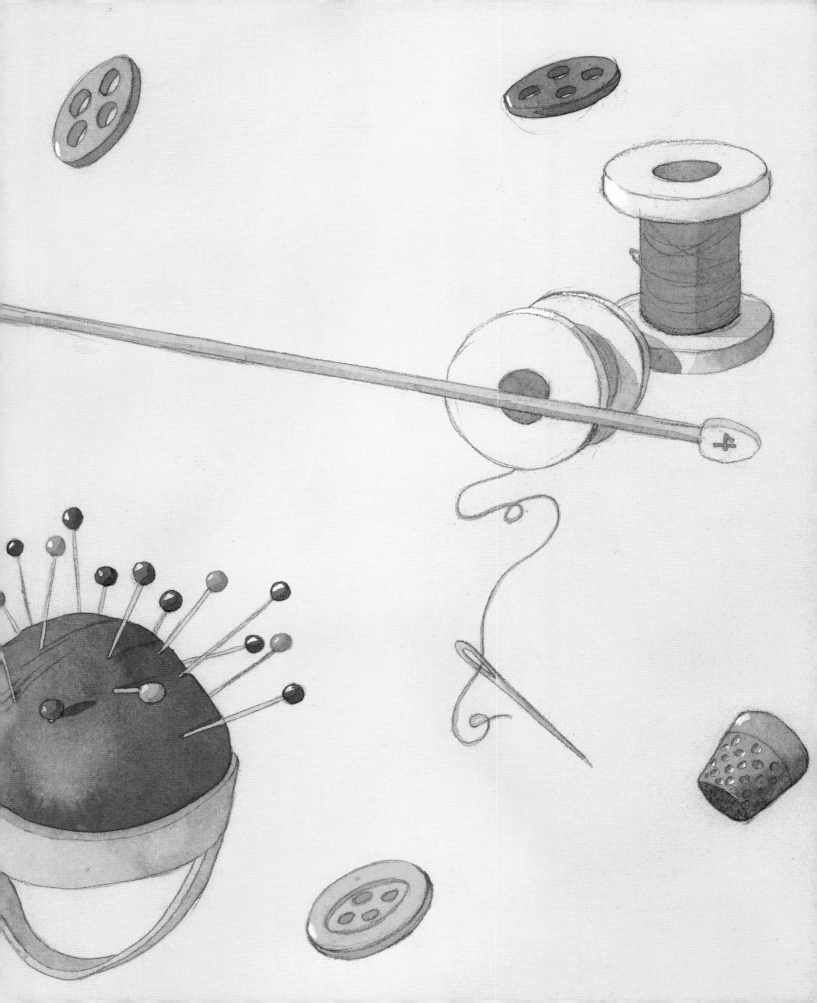

For Léa,
my little mouse
NW

For Didine
QG

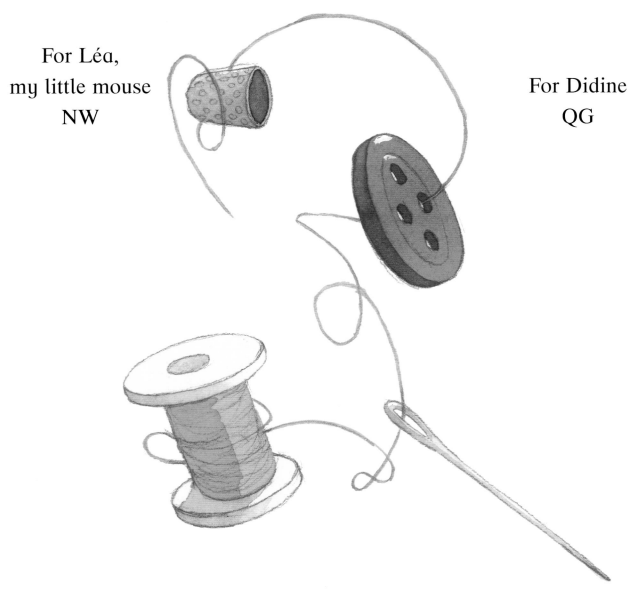

MYRIAD BOOKS LIMITED
35 Bishopsthorpe Road, London SE26 4PA

First published in 2004 by
MIJADE PUBLICATIONS
16-18, rue de l'Ouvrage
5000 Namur-Belgium

© Nadine Walter, 2004
© Quentin Gréban, 2004
Translation Lisa Pritchard

ISBN 1 905606 27 3

Printed in China

Lizzie's List

Nadine Walter
Quentin Gréban

MYRIAD BOOKS LIMITED

Lizzie loved making clothes.

She didn't need much: just a tiny scrap of material and a little thread. A couple of hours later, she had made a lovely coat.

Lizzie worked so hard her friends and neighbours soon had all the clothes they could wear.

Lizzie needed to find someone who would buy her beautiful clothes or she would not have enough money for food.

One windy autumn day, Lizzie set off to find new customers. She knocked on every door she found.

"No thank you, Lizzie," said Marvin Mouse. "Don't you remember? You made us lots of lovely clothes last year!"

Hector Mole didn't need anything either.

But he did have an idea. "Why don't you talk to the big animals in the woods, Lizzie?"

Lizzie sighed: "They are all so BIG, Hector, and I am very, very small. Or else they live high up a tree, or down a deep dark hole. Or they are really scary."

The little mouse went home feeling sad. She was very hungry but there wasn't much left to eat.

The next morning Lizzie was sitting on her
sewing machine, trying to think what to do.

Suddenly there was a knock at
the door.

Hector was very excited. "I've had a good idea! Here's my friend Will Squirrel. He needs a new jumper to keep him warm. Grab your tape measure and climb up onto my shoulders – then you'll be tall enough to take his measurements!"

What a great idea! Now it was easy for Lizzie to measure the squirrel's back and arms.

She jumped down and quickly got out her knitting needles. CLICKETY-CLICK! CLICKETY-CLICK! She knitted all through the night.

When Will Squirrel saw his new jumper in the morning
he was very happy. "I love it, Lizzie."
He put it on right away.

Bobby Badger stopped to admire the jumper.
"That's beautiful, Lizzie!" he said. "Would
you make me a new coat please?"

Lizzie got out her tape measure and climbed up onto Hector's shoulders.
But she couldn't quite reach all the way up to Bobby's neck.

Will Squirrel said, "Don't worry! Come on Hector, you stand on my
shoulders and then Lizzie will be able to reach."

A couple of days later they all went back to see Bobby Badger and he tried on his new yellow coat.

It was amazing. He felt great. Everyone he knew agreed that his coat was very smart.

Even Ludo Wolf called out: "NICE COAT, BOBBY!" as he went off to hunt for his supper.

"G-G-G-G-GOOD WORK," said Winnie
Woodpecker. "If my feet weren't
so C-C-COLD
I'd give you
a C-C-CLAP."

"Would you like me to knit you some
socks?" Lizzie called up. "Just come
down and I'll get out my tape
measure."

"I don't like being
down there," said Winnie.

"Never mind," said Lizzie.

She climbed onto Hector's
shoulders… and Hector climbed
up onto Will Squirrel's back…
and Will climbed up onto
Bobby Badger's back…
and now Lizzie could just
reach up to Winnie's feet.

Higher up the tree, Ollie Owl was snoozing.
When he opened his eyes he saw Winnie
Woodpecker's new green socks.
"WHOO-OO made those for you,
Winnie? They look really warm."

"Lizzie made them for me,"
Winnie replied.

Ollie called down to Lizzie.
"I need a long woolly scarf to
keep me warm in the winter."

Winnie Woodpecker lifted Lizzie up onto the owl's
branch. She started knitting and soon she
was wrapping the new scarf round Ollie's
shoulders.

"Thank you, Lizzie. That makes me feel snug and warm,"
said the owl.

When Lizzie got down the tree a queue of animals were waiting to see her. Everyone wanted her to make something for them…

The weasel wanted a new dress.

The field mouse needed a hat.

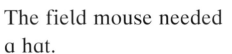

The chaffinch was thrilled with his socks.

And the rabbits just loved their dungarees.

Lizzie was very, very busy, cutting and stitching, sewing and knitting. She worked and worked. Sometimes she was so tired that she fell asleep with her needle in her paw.

One day Edgar Beaver called her over to his dam.

Winnie Woodpecker held a stick in his mouth, and Lizzie held on very tight. She didn't want to fall into the river.

Edgar said, "I need new pyjamas."

To be on the safe side, Lizzie made him some waterproof pyjamas.

When Harriet Cow wanted a new dressing gown, Lizzie called all her friends to come and help. Harriet was very big. "But how am I going to know where to put the buttons?" she said.

Hector had an idea. "If Harriet holds one end of this rope… and Ollie grabs the other end… then you can slide down under Harriet's chin."

It was a really good idea, until Harriet started chewing the rope. Lizzie swung here… AND THERE… and back again. She was getting a bit dizzy. But she held on tight!

When Harriet wore her new dressing gown she knew she was the best dressed cow in the field.

Then one morning, Hector came to see Lizzie. He was rather worried. "You've got another customer…
it's Ludo Wolf."

"WHAT!" exclaimed Lizzie. "But… but… he'll gobble me up!" she trembled.

"He really needs a new hat. And if he doesn't get it, he'll gobble you up anyway," said Hector.

Lizzie gulped and set off to see Ludo Wolf.

"I'll only make you a hat if you promise not to gobble me up," she said.

"And you mustn't gobble up my friends, either," she said. Ludo sighed and then nodded his head.

Bobby Badger stood nervously next to Ludo Wolf.

Will Squirrel stood nervously on Bobby's shoulders.

Hector stood nervously on Will's shoulders.

Finally, Lizzie stood nervously on Hector's shoulders and started measuring.

When she stood on Ludo's nose, she gulped. "Remember your promises!" she whispered.

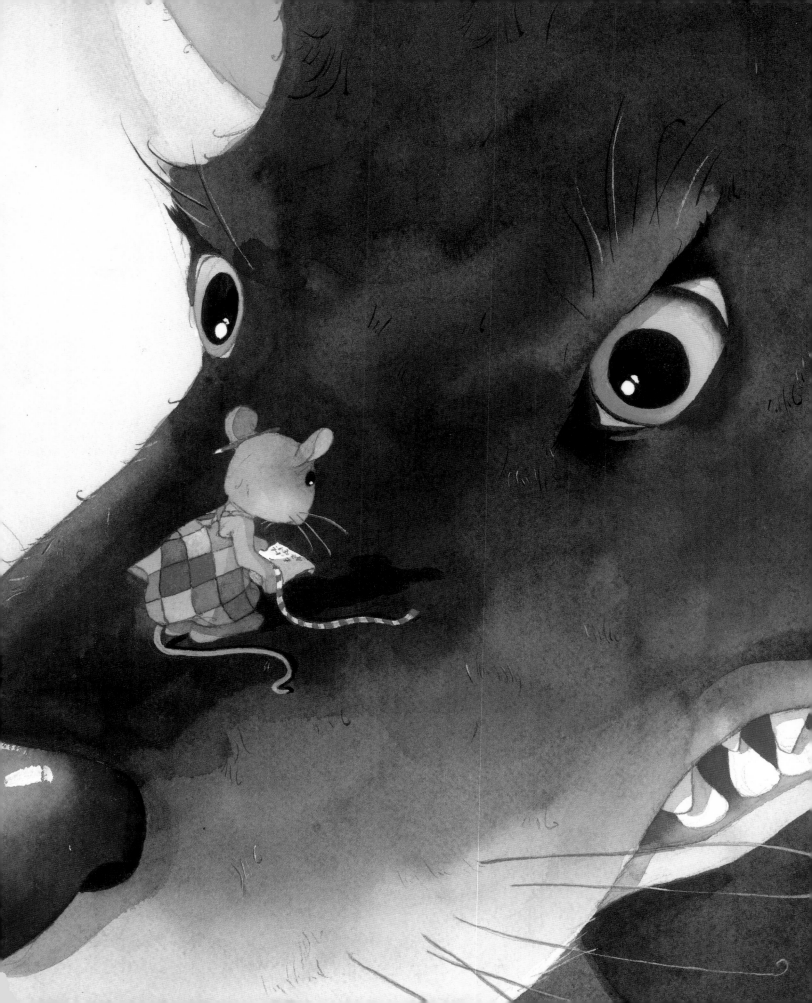

Lizzie was very careful when she wrote down Ludo's measurements. She didn't want to make any mistakes or he might forget his promises.

When Lizzie had finished the hat she brought it to Ludo. He tried it on.

Lizzie and her friends were very worried when Ludo took it off again.
"OH NO!" said Lizzie.
"He doesn't like it at all!"

But Ludo wasn't cross. He loved his hat. He swept it to the side and made a dramatic bow.

"Miss Lizzie Mouse! I congratulate you on making a truly magnificent hat! From now on you will make all my hats."

All the other animals breathed a big sigh of relief. "THREE CHEERS FOR LIZZIE!" said Hector.

And they all joined in. "HURRAY! HURRAY! HURRAY! Well done, Lizzie!"

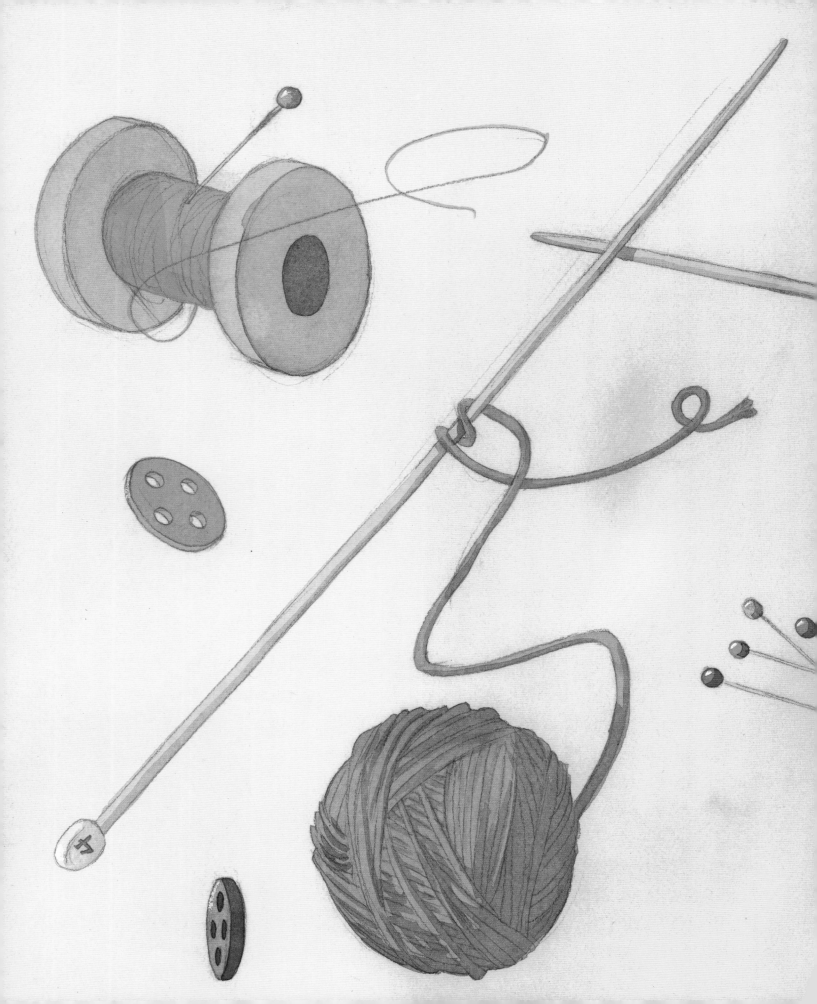

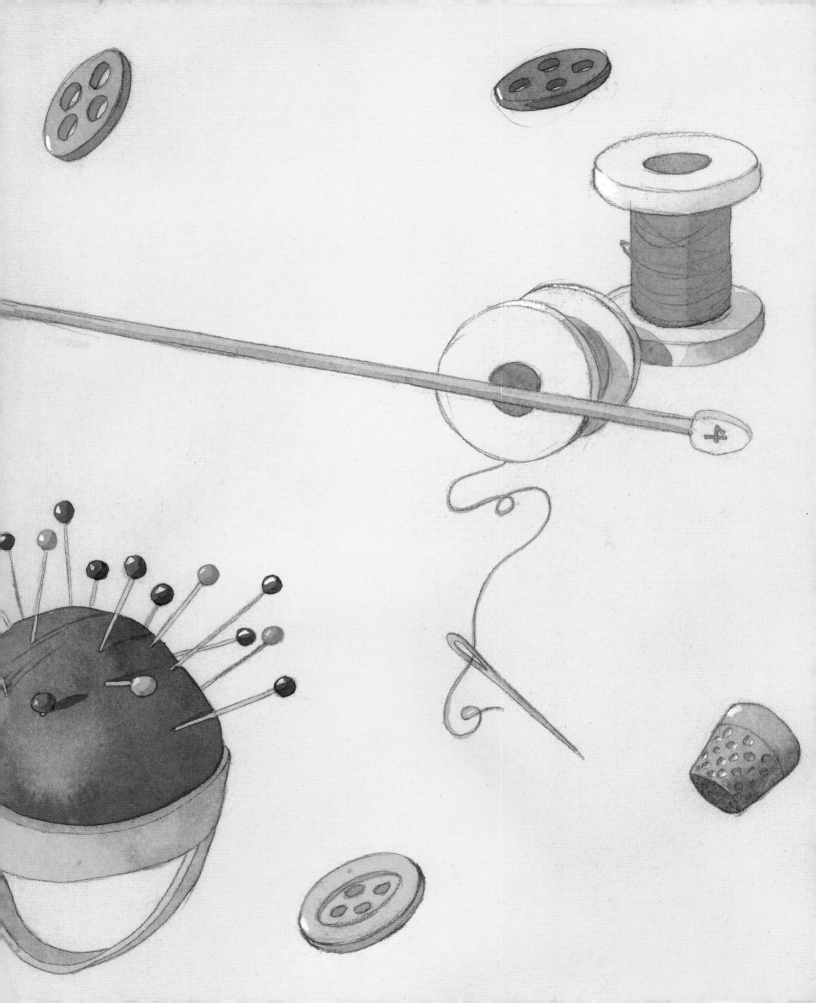